**HOPSCOTCH ADVENTURES**

# Robin

## and the **Butcher**

by Damian Harvey and Martin Remphry

FRANKLIN WATTS
LONDON • SYDNEY

First published in 2009 by
Franklin Watts
338 Euston Road
London
NW1 3BH

Franklin Watts Australia
Level 17/207 Kent Street
Sydney
NSW 2000

Text © Damian Harvey 2009
Illustrations © Martin Remphry 2009

A CIP catalogue record for this book is available
from the British Library.

ISBN 978 0 7496 8555 3 (hbk)
ISBN 978 0 7496 8568 3 (pbk)

**Series Editor:** Jackie Hamley
**Series Advisor:** Dr Barrie Wade
**Series Designer:** Peter Scoulding

Printed in China

Franklin Watts is a division of
Hachette Children's Books,
an Hachette UK company
www.hachette.co.uk

Robin Hood and Little John were
lazing on a branch when they heard
a horse coming along the road.

"Come on," said Robin. "It might be a rich duke with a heavy purse." As the horse got closer, Robin could see it was not a rich duke.

It was a butcher, and he looked
very miserable indeed.

"Why are you so unhappy on this
fine day?" asked Robin Hood.

"It might be a fine day to you," said the butcher, "but the greedy Sheriff takes so much of my money that I cannot afford to feed my family. So today I will have to sell both my meat and my horse."

"That Sheriff needs to be taught a lesson," said Robin. "Rest here, my friend, and I will go to the market and sell your meat."

Robin Hood put on the butcher's
hat and apron, then set off to
Nottingham market.

At the market, lots of people
bought their meat from Robin
because he sold it cheaply.

The other butchers were amazed.
"This is *very* strange," they said.
"How can he afford to sell his
meat so cheaply?"

Even the Sheriff of Nottingham
heard about the mysterious
butcher and came to see
what was going on.

"This *is* very strange," agreed the Sheriff. "This butcher must be a foolish, rich man who wants to waste all his money."

The other butchers were not happy with Robin because the people had bought all their meat from him and none from them.

"Don't be angry my friends," said Robin. "Come with me and I will buy a fine dinner for us all."

While Robin and the butchers ate
and drank, the Sheriff smiled.
He thought this was a chance
to make himself even richer.

"You must have a lot of deer
and cattle to be selling your
meat so cheaply," said the Sheriff.
"I have many beasts," said Robin.
"Hundreds of them."

"Perhaps you would sell some of your fine beasts to me," said the Sheriff.

"Of course," said Robin Hood.

"Come and see them for yourself."

The Sheriff took three hundred
gold coins, saddled his best horse,
and followed Robin Hood.

When they got close to Sherwood Forest, the Sheriff started to worry. "We should be careful. The outlaw, Robin Hood, hides here," he said. "Don't worry about Robin Hood," said Robin brightly. "Look! There are my beasts."

The Sheriff looked at the animals grazing in the fields. Then he frowned. "These are not yours," he said. "They belong to the King."

"If they belong to the King,
then they belong to everyone,"
said Robin Hood.

Before the Sheriff could say
another word, Robin blew his
horn three times.

Little John and the rest of Robin's
merry men came out of the forest
and surrounded the Sheriff.

"The kind Sheriff has brought us a bag of gold and a fine new horse," said Robin Hood. The merry men laughed and cheered.

That night, the butcher went home with a fine new horse, a pocket full of gold and a smile on his face.

The Sheriff rode angrily back
to Nottingham.

Put these pictures in the correct order.
Which event do you think is most important?
Now try writing the story in your own words!

# Puzzle 2

**1.** I have to sell my horse now.

**2.** Let me take your horse to the market.

**3.** What a stupid butcher.

**4.** That Sheriff is in for a surprise!

**5.** I can buy his beasts and make lots of money!

**6.** My family has nothing left to eat.

Choose the correct speech bubbles for each character. Can you think of any others? Turn over to find the answers.

# Answers

## Puzzle 1

The correct order is: 1e, 2f, 3d, 4a, 5c, 6b

## Puzzle 2

Robin Hood: 2, 4

The butcher: 1, 6

The Sheriff: 3, 5

## Look out for more Hopscotch Adventures:

### TALES OF KING ARTHUR

**1. The Sword in the Stone**
ISBN 978 0 7496 6694 1

**2. Arthur the King**
ISBN 978 0 7496 6695 8

**3. The Round Table**
ISBN 978 0 7496 6697 2

**4. Sir Lancelot and the Ice Castle**
ISBN 978 0 7496 6698 9

**5. Sir Gawain and the Green Knight**
ISBN 978 0 7496 8557 7*
ISBN 978 0 7496 8569 0

**6. Sir Galahad and the Holy Grail**
ISBN 978 0 7496 8558 4*
ISBN 978 0 7496 8570 6

### TALES OF ROBIN HOOD

**Robin and the Knight**
ISBN 978 0 7496 6699 6

**Robin and the Monk**
ISBN 978 0 7496 6700 9

**Robin and the Silver Arrow**
ISBN 978 0 7496 6703 0

**Robin and the Friar**
ISBN 978 0 7496 6702 3

**Robin and the Butcher**
ISBN 978 0 7496 8555 3*
ISBN 978 0 7496 8568 3

**Robin and Maid Marian**
ISBN 978 0 7496 8556 0*
ISBN 978 0 7496 8567 6

### TALES OF SINBAD THE SAILOR

**Sinbad and the Ogre**
ISBN 978 0 7496 8559 1*
ISBN 978 0 7496 8571 3

**Sinbad and the Whale**
ISBN 978 0 7496 8553 9*
ISBN 978 0 7496 8565 2

**Sinbad and the Diamond Valley**
ISBN 978 0 7496 8554 6*
ISBN 978 0 7496 8566 9

**Sinbad and the Monkeys**
ISBN 978 0 7496 8560 7*
ISBN 978 0 7496 8572 0

For more *Hopscotch Adventures* and other *Hopscotch* stories, visit:
www.franklinwatts.co.uk

* hardback